Applesauce
Weather

❧

Applesauce
Weather

Helen Frost

illustrated by Amy June Bates

CANDLEWICK PRESS

Text copyright © 2016 by Helen Frost
Illustrations copyright © 2016 by Amy June Bates

First paperback edition 2018

Library of Congress Catalog Card Number 2016940426
ISBN 978-0-7636-7576-9 (hardcover)
ISBN 978-1-5362-0361-5 (paperback)

18 19 20 21 22 23 BVG 10 9 8 7 6 5 4 3 2 1

Printed in Berryville, VA, U.S.A.

This book was typeset in Horley Old Style.
The illustrations were done in oil-based pencil.

Candlewick Press
99 Dover Street
Somerville, Massachusetts 02144

visit us at www.candlewick.com

The Apple Tree

A house beside an orchard
at the edge of a small town,
a bench beneath an apple tree,
an old barn falling down.

A long road comes from somewhere,
goes to an unknown end—
this story tells what happens
between here and that first bend.

Faith

Today is the day I've been waiting for: the first apple
fell from the tree. Uncle Arthur will be here
      sometime today—
        just wait and see.

I pick up the apple, check for worms,
wipe off a smudge of dirt,
and polish it on a corner
      of my soft red shirt.

Should I bite the juicy bruised place,
      warm from noontime sun,
        or take the first bite from the crispy side?
Neither one—
I'll save it. He will be here soon.

Even though Aunt Lucy won't
      make applesauce this year,
        when Uncle Arthur comes, he'll find
        me waiting here.

Peter

My sister is ridiculous.
Silly. Superstitious.
Uncle Arthur lives in town,
a two-hour drive away from us.
How could he possibly know
when the first apple falls
from our tree?

Faith

Mom tells us to remember
      it used to be
      Aunt Lucy's apple tree—
this house was her house
      when she was a child.
Mom says, *I don't believe*
      he'll come this year
      without her.
I think she's wrong,
      but she goes on:
Uncle Arthur might still need
      a little more time to grieve.

Uncle Arthur

A vee of geese high overhead,
a sunflower high as a house.
A smell in the air — if Lucy were here,
she'd breathe it deep. She'd smile wide.
That's all it would take — we'd be on our way:
Applesauce weather, she'd say.

Faith

I sit on this bench and wait and wait,
holding the apple, not taking a bite,
and Aunt Lucy's song starts singing itself to me:
> *I planted a seed from an apple I bought.*
> *I started my tree in a little pot*
> *when I was a girl no bigger than you.*
> *As I grew taller, my tree grew, too.*

Uncle Arthur

Lucy and I would set out in the morning
on the day we knew the first apple would fall.
I'd sit on the bench with Peter and Faith
while Lucy filled her pail.
And there on that bench by the apple tree—
oh, the tales I could tell.

How can I go this year without her?

(Are they expecting me?)

Peter

Supper's almost ready,
and still my sister sits,
holding that apple,
watching the road,
like it's a scientific fact
that the first apple
to fall from this tree
will somehow act
like a magnet, pulling
Uncle Arthur home to us.
It's obvious by now
he isn't coming.
Can't she see?

Faith

Mom comes out to call me in for supper,
sits down beside me, runs her fingers through my hair.

She looks down the road and takes a deep breath.
I'm sorry, Faith. It looks like
> *Uncle Arthur's not coming this year.*

Peter

Faith lets Mom drag her in for supper,
insists on sitting where I usually sit—
facing the window, watching the road.
All through supper, she pesters, like this:
Grandma was Aunt Lucy's sister, so
that makes Uncle Arthur our great-uncle.
                    Right?
Mom says, *Yes. He's your great-uncle by marriage.*

And then Faith starts to beg:
Come on, tell us, Mom—he must have told you—
what really happened to Uncle Arthur's finger?
Mom gives us the same
not-an-answer
as always:
You tell me and we'll both know, she says.

Faith

I don't care if it's dark out. I could stay
here all night long.
The moon in the sky, half full. The crickets
cricking their song.

What's that? Behind the crickets, a distant
motor sound . . .
and now, lights shine around the bend—
there is a car on the road!

Peter

Like a puppy—like a whole litter
of puppies—my sister runs
from bench to house to road.
See? I told you! Look! He's here!

The car pulls up—it's him, all right.
He pops the trunk and grabs
a suitcase, fast. I picture how
he'd always let Aunt Lucy
do the hugging while he'd be looking
everywhere but us: *Why'd you paint
the shed that ugly shade of green?
Duke's getting old—never knew dogs'
beards got gray.* Luckily, he brought
two suitcases. *Hey, let me get that!* I say.
I grab his other suitcase. Let Mom
and Dad and Faith stand there and try
to figure what to do with all those
extra
empty
arms.

Faith

All day, Mom's been saying, *Don't expect*
him, Faith. Try not to get your hopes up.
Chances are, he won't come this year.

But where
       did this gingerbread come from,
            with the warm lemon sauce
                 he loves?

It's not like it could magically appear
the minute Uncle Arthur
came walking through the door.
Mom had to buy the lemons
       and bake the gingerbread
            so she could cut this piece
            for Uncle Arthur
            and he could ask for more.

Lucy's Song

Like brother and sister, we played and fought—
Arthur lived down the road from me.
When the seedling outgrew its little pot,
we planted it here. We chose this spot.
From each of our windows, we could see
the seedling becoming an apple tree.

Uncle Arthur

I look out the window that used to be Lucy's:
there's a light in the window
that used to be mine.
But nobody
flashes
one,
four,
three
(*I love you,*
we'd flash, that summer
when we were fifteen). Tonight,
in this darkness, it's only the moon, old
and lonely, that seems to be taking a shine to me.

Faith

Every year, I ask Uncle Arthur,
    What happened to your finger?
Every year, he holds out his hands.
One. Two. Three, he counts.
Four. Five. Six.
Seven. Eight.
    Nine?
Now, where, he asks, *could that last*
    finger
    be?

Faith

Three years ago, when I was six
and Peter was seven, we asked,
the same as we always do:
> *What happened to your finger, Uncle Arthur?*

He thought for a minute,
>   polished an apple,
>   looked down the road for a minute or two.

Well, he said, *it was like this. You know
Lucy's sugar molasses cookies?*
I love those cookies.
>   *Yes,* I said, *that cinnamon smell,*
>   *even before they go into the oven,*
>   *and then when they're warm . . . mmmm, yes.*
I could just about taste them — I knew.

Well, maybe, Uncle Arthur said,
>   *you'll understand why I did*
>   *what I did. I'm sure neither of you*
>   *would do such a thing,*
>   *but I couldn't resist. I tried to snitch*

just a tiny bit — hardly even a bite — of that
sugar molasses cookie dough.

My face got hot. I looked away. Had he
seen what I'd done that very day?

> *What happened?* I whispered.
> *I was quick,* Uncle Arthur went on,
> *and remember, it was only a tiny bit.*
> *Of course I thought Lucy*
> *wouldn't see — but did you know*
> *she has eyes in the back of her head?*

Peter protested, *She does not!*

Uncle Arthur raised an eyebrow and said,
> *Well, how else did I get caught*
> *in the act that long-ago day? Yes,*
> he went on, *it happened like this:*
> *quick as a flash, before I could get*
> *that dough in my mouth, Lucy picked up*

her shears — they were sharp as a knife —
and she snipped my finger off.

Yes, she snipped this finger right clean off.
And I haven't seen it since.

He held out his hand, and I touched the place
where his finger should be, the stump
of the finger that used to be there.

Peter rolled his eyes halfway back in his head.
Aunt Lucy gave a little snort.
Oh, Arthur, she said.

He gave her a twinkly, wrinkly smile.
They chuckled together,
and that's how I knew
      that story couldn't
      possibly be true.

Lucy's Song

At first we both grew as fast as the tree.
Then I grew taller than Arthur
and the tree grew taller than me.
Each year it stretched its branches high,
past my window, into the sky.
One year it gave us an apple to share—
the next year it gave us a pie.

Faith

Last year, Aunt Lucy slept most of the time,
      in a bed we moved near the window.
Instead of going out to the apple tree,
      Uncle Arthur sat quietly by her side.
We were quiet, too; it didn't seem right
      to beg for stories at a time like that.
But one day a breeze
      came through the window, swept
      back the curtains, and let in some light.

Uncle Arthur turned to Peter and me.
      Have I ever told you about the time
      I was out in a rowboat with Lucy?
No, he hadn't. I shook my head.
      Oh, she was beautiful that day—
      her hair down her back,
      in a long black braid,
      her red hat perched on her head.
         We sat in the boat . . .

His voice got funny. I wasn't sure if he'd say any more.

Well, he finally went on,
wouldn't you know,
a breeze came along
and lifted that hat
right off Lucy's head!

Away it flew! It came down in the water—
I rowed as fast as the wind,
then faster!
I reached down to get Lucy's hat—and then,
what do you think, Peter and Faith?
Who wanted that hat as much as we did?

How would we know? We weren't even born
when he and Aunt Lucy were young like that!

I could tell that Peter was torn—not believing
        it really happened but wanting
        to know who was after the hat.

Uncle Arthur waited. He tried not to smile.
        Who? I finally had to ask.

Well, he said, *a hungry old crocodile*
swam to our boat, opened his jaws,
and grabbed Lucy's hat.

> *Just like that, it was under the water,*
> *its long red ribbons streaming behind.*
> *Tell me, now: what could I do?*

Why would a crocodile want a red hat?
Before I could ask, Uncle Arthur went on:

> *Did he want that hat for his crocodile dinner?*
> *Or was it a gift for his favorite girl?*

WHO GOT THE HAT?

I had to know, but I couldn't shout—
    Aunt Lucy was resting, so
    What happened next? I whispered.
Uncle Arthur gave me a gentle smile.
    Don't you worry, he said.
        I got that hat back for my Lucy.

Aunt Lucy turned toward his voice.

    But I'm sorry to say,
    that rascal,
    that toothy old crocodile,
    swam off
    with my finger
    that day.
    And . . .

I looked at Peter; he looked at me.
    We knew what came next.

I haven't seen it since.

The smallest smile
    crossed Aunt Lucy's face.
She opened her eyes,
    then closed them again.

Uncle Arthur took her hand
    and looked at her for a long, long time.

I wondered then: Was he telling
    that story to Peter and me
    or to his beautiful black-haired,
        lovely white-haired
            Lucy?

Lucy's Song

When Arthur built this bench for me,
so I could sit under the apple tree,
he drew it on paper, planned it out:
the angle of sun in late afternoon,
the size the tree would be as it grew.
Those were the things he thought about
before either of us thought I love you.

Uncle Arthur

It was easy to think of stories
when I knew I had Lucy's ear.
She'd listen, and they'd come
to me, and some of them,
so Lucy said, were pretty good.

Now when I try to listen,
all I seem to hear
is that tired old bullfrog
down in the pond,
up to its eyeballs in mud.

Peter

After breakfast
Uncle Arthur pushes back his chair,
picks up his walking stick,
and heads out the door.

Faith follows, grabs his hand.
Nothing else to do —
guess I might as well go, too.

We walk to the old bench
beside the apple tree.
Faith and Uncle Arthur sit down.
As for me,
I grab a low branch,
  swing by my knees,
  and listen
  to the buzzing bees.

Uncle Arthur

Are the children expecting a story from me?
They're not asking — perhaps
they can see the empty place
where my stories would be
if Lucy were here to hear them.

Faith sits beside me, taking my hand
(my thumb-and-three-and-a-half-fingers hand).
Is she old enough to understand how things
can go missing and never be found?
Too much silence can make a deafening sound.

Faith

I've walked down the road with Uncle Arthur every day,
three days in a row and still no stories. What if
he has no stories left? Maybe he's told them all,
and it's up to me to tell him stories now.

Look, I say, pointing to a flash of blue, *there goes
Peter on his bike again.* (Third time he's gone
past in half an hour.) *Sure enough,* says Uncle Arthur.
His feet up on the handlebars. I wonder why.

I start wondering, too, and the next time Peter flashes by,
I tell my guess to Uncle Arthur: *Peter likes a girl named Rose,
who lives in the same house you lived in, all those years ago.
Maybe her room is the same room that used to be yours.*

*I bet she watches out the window, just like you did,
when Aunt Lucy was a girl. That's why Peter rides his bike
with his feet up on the handlebars like that.*
Uncle Arthur cracks a smile. *Is that a fact?* he asks.

Peter

Faith and Uncle Arthur
walking down the road
acting like they know something
I don't know.

Uncle Arthur always
has a story up his sleeve.
No end to the nonsense
he gets Faith to believe.

They keep looking at me.
Then they smile together, like
they're making up some lies
about a boy on a bike.

Uncle Arthur

I was the same age Peter is now
the summer I got this knife. Never thinking
I'd use it to carve those initials, never dreaming
(far from it — what ten-year-old would?)
that someday Lucy would be my wife.

Five years later, we carved in the tree
A.A. and *L.P.* So crisp and clear.
It's hard to see now, but if you get close
to where the trunk split in the storm
last year — yes, here it is, I'll show the children —
Peter and Faith, look here.

Peter

I study the initials—
thick scars on the tree trunk.
How did you carve this? I ask.

Uncle Arthur looks at me funny.
He puts his hand in his pocket.
(Oh! I didn't mean it like that.

He can do anything anyone can
with that missing-finger hand.)
I mean . . . I begin.

With a knife, he says, looking off
down the road. *We carved our initials
with a good sharp knife.*

Faith

When lightning struck the apple tree,
a branch fell down and we pushed it aside.
Tall grass grew up and covered it.
I forgot it was even there. Now Peter
drags it out of the grass. He sits
on a tree stump, holding the branch,
trying to carve with his orange knife,
the plastic-handled pocketknife
he won last summer at the county fair.

Uncle Arthur

Here comes an old memory
walking down the road,
like a peddler
pushing a heavy load.

I'll walk out to meet him,
see what he has to sell—
a hammer, and a pound
of two-inch nails,
a cooking pot, and
a new tin pail.
Somewhere in the mix,
I might have found
the beginning of a strange
new tale to tell.

Faith

Uncle Arthur has the start
of a smile on his face — a tiny twinkle
in his eyes, a little crinkle
near the corners of his mouth.

Maybe this will be the day
we can ask him,
maybe this will be the year
we'll finally know —
     What really happened to that finger?

Faith

I found a stick Peter tossed aside,
with his initials carved all over it.
P. and C. Peter Cassidy.
I bet it's hard to make that P—
a little circle has to meet a straight line,
and all he has to carve with
is his cheap, dull knife.

Look—one of these P's has an extra leg!
Did he make a mistake, or
is he trying to make
an R for Rose?
Yes—here's a T!
Peter likes Rosie Timmons. Oooh!
It's true, all right.
I wonder if she likes him, too.

Uncle Arthur

Peter's trying to carve a stick
that fell off the apple tree.
Maybe I should give him
a little advice:
> Practice for a while
> on a bar of Ivory soap.
> Find a softer piece of wood.
> Take your time.
> You have your whole life
> to get the details right.

Peter

Uncle Arthur looks over my shoulder.
That's a pretty good dog
you got there, son.
I don't answer, and he goes on:
I used to practice
on a bar of soap. (So did I—
when I was four years old.)
I get up and walk away.
(I don't tell him
I was carving a grizzly bear.)

Lucy's Song

The first time we kissed, we were standing here,
apple blossoms perfuming the air.
I tucked a blossom behind my ear.
Arthur pushed back a strand of my hair,
and in all the years since, we never missed
that first apple-blossom kiss each year.

Faith

It's applesauce weather for sure today,
apples ripening faster
than we can pick them.
>   *Come on, Uncle Arthur,* I say,
>   *let's walk down to the apple tree.*

I grab Aunt Lucy's apple pail,
which seems to make Uncle Arthur smile.
>   *Peter,* he calls,
>   *are you coming, too?*
>   *I may have a story for Faith and you.*

Peter

Uncle Arthur has this thing he does,
thumping the stump of his missing finger
to say, *Come on over here and sit down.*
Usually it's Faith who runs right over,
but she's busy picking apples now —
the ones that fell to the ground this morning,
the ones on the branches, about to fall.

So I'm the one sitting beside him today
when he clears his throat and says, *Well* . . .
like it's some kind of question I don't know
the answer to — don't even know
it's a question at all.

Faith figures it out; she hears what he means.
She sets down her pail and comes over.
She sits on the bench, takes his hand in hers,
asks what we've all been not-asking this year:
      Uncle Arthur, she looks up and says,
      what happened to your finger?

Uncle Arthur looks down the road
to Rosie's house, where he used to live,
long ago when he was a boy.
It seems like he's traveling past it now,
around the curve where the road goes on,
beyond what we can see from here.

He glances at Faith, then looks at me.
Makes a sound that starts somewhere
down in his throat, like he's waiting
for words,

               and here they come.

Uncle Arthur

I take a deep breath before I begin.
> *It happened like this, a long time ago.*
> *I can still see him like it was yesterday,*
> *a man we called Peddler Joe.*
> *Pushing his cart, he came every year—*
> *around that bend in the road.*

Peter tries to look like he's not listening.
Faith sits beside me, swinging her feet.
She looks at me, her eyes big as plates,
then hands me an apple from Lucy's pail
and waits while I take a few bites.

> *One summer—oh, I remember it well,*
> *I was just the age you are now, Peter,*
> *though not quite as big (I was always small)*
> *and not half as smart—maybe you can tell me*
> *what I should have done, because I've never been sure*
> *if I did the right thing back then.*

Peter

How much of that apple
is he going to eat
before he tells us more?

He glances at me, takes three
more bites, then chews
and swallows the apple core.

Uncle Arthur

It's a good day — yes, it is — a hazy
late-summer, thundercloud day —
to be telling this crazy old story.

> *Let me tell you about Peddler Joe.*
> *We'd hear him coming well before*
> *he rounded that bend in the road.*
> *He'd play a tune on his mouth organ,*
> *ring a bell on his cart, and all of us children*
> *would run out to meet him, everyone curious —*
> *what did he bring us? The lucky*
> *among us had coins in our pockets,*
> *pennies and nickels we'd saved all year*
> *for jump ropes and marbles,*
> *gumdrops and gobstoppers, Cracker Jack,*
> *licorice sticks, root-beer barrels.*

Faith takes my hand, turns it over, and asks,
Uncle Arthur, is this going to be
> *the true story of what really happened?*

Now it looks like Peter is listening, too.

I'm coming to that. I'll get there, I say.
This might be a two-day tale.
Even three.

Uncle Arthur

Long ago, I go on, *on a day like this,*
I was lying in a clover patch,
watching the clouds change shape —
much as you are now, Peter —
when Peddler Joe came pushing his cart
around that bend in the road.
My pockets were empty,
but I was still glad when
I heard the ring of his bell.
I ran out to meet him, and here's how
he greeted me: "Hello, Arthur Armitage."
Now, I was surprised he knew my name —
it was over a year since I'd seen him.
I held out my hand the way I'd been taught,
said, "Hello, Peddler Joe. How are you today?"
He answered, "I'm fine," as he stretched
out his hand. He watched me as I shook it.

Now, he had everything in that cart,
anything anyone wanted and more —
but I had never noticed before
what Peddler Joe was missing.

I stared at his hand and checked to be sure.
One, two . . . Yes, it was true: Peddler Joe
had only three fingers
where he should have had four.

Peter sits up straight. *Which finger was missing?*
I hold up the stump
of my index finger.
  Well, wouldn't you know,
  it was this one, I say.
  Just like you! Faith gasps.
  Not quite, I remind her.
  Peddler Joe had three fingers
  on his right hand. She nods.
  And a thumb, Peter adds.
Faith takes my hand in her two hands.
  And you, she says,
    have three and a half.

Faith

That's enough for now, says Uncle Arthur.
Time for an old man to go take a nap.
He picks up an apple and walks up the path,
leaving Peter and me by the apple tree.

We're quiet, thinking about Peddler Joe
as we fill Aunt Lucy's old apple pail.
I'm on the ground; Peter's climbing high,
tossing down hard-to-reach apples to me.

When he climbs back down, I ask, *Could it be
contagious, Peter? You know—could a boy catch
a missing finger from an old man?* It's stupid, I know,
but still . . . Peter touches his own right hand.

Sure hope not, he says, *cause that would mean . . .*
Then his face turns red and he says, *No way.*
He shakes a branch, and apples go flying,
like when a dog comes out of a lake,
shaking water all over the place.

Lucy's Song

After we married and moved away,
we came back to visit, and then to stay.
We sold Arthur's house and moved in here,
bringing his bed and his favorite chair.

We were happy together, year after year.

When we could no longer climb the stairs,
we moved into town — life is easier there.
In the years since then, it's been good to see
Faith and Peter enjoying the apple tree.

Faith

Fierce rain, wet grass,
thunder and lightning
keep us indoors today. We sit
at the old kitchen table
around a bushel of apples.
Uncle Arthur peels, Dad cores,
I cut. Mom stands at the stove
and stirs the applesauce pot.
Peter comes in with a piece of soft pine,
and sits on a stool, whittling something.
> Mosquito?
> Bird? Flying fish?
> This time no one
> tries to guess.

Uncle Arthur

The apple peelings are piling up.
Faith looks at me and says, *Tell us more,*
Uncle Arthur. Tell us the rest. What happened
       with Peddler Joe back then?

I pick up another apple to peel.
Ah, yes, I say. *Where was I, now?*
Asleep at our feet, Duke thumps his tail.
Remember? He was missing a finger, Faith prompts.
Almost like you, Peter adds, *but not quite.*

I tell them, *Here's the thing you should know*
about old Peddler Joe:
       When his cart was light,
       his heart was bright.
       And that day, his cart
       was pretty near empty
       as he set off down the road.
       He'd sold bracelets and blankets,
       flashlights and firecrackers,
       nutcrackers and . . . I pause to remember.
Knives? Peter asks. (He's getting ahead of me.)

Ah, yes, he had sold a few
knives that day—butter knives,
kitchen knives, knives with bone handles,
carving knives, paring knives.
But what did I care for those? I wanted
a knife I could keep in my pocket,
a knife that would open and close.
So sharp it would slice through the hardest wood—
apple wood, hickory, maple, and oak.
If I had such a knife, I'd be an artist.
I could carve birds that would practically fly.
Yes, I thought, I would carve a bear
that would scare the wits out of my sister.
(Peter looks up at me, glances at Faith.)
Oh, how I wanted a pocketknife.
Shiny and sharp when I opened it,
snug and safe when I snapped it shut
and slipped it into my pocket.

And then, as I was longing and wishing,
that long-ago afternoon,
Peddler Joe reached down deep in his cart,
and what do you think he pulled out?
What do you think he took from its case
and held out to me that day?

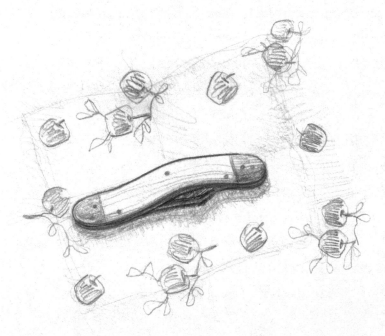

Peter

I answer Uncle Arthur's question: *A pocketknife.*
It's obvious.
> But it makes no sense.
> Why would a peddler take out a knife
> and show it to Arthur Armitage, even though he knew
> the boy had no money to buy it?

That's right, Uncle Arthur says. *A sharp and shiny*
silver knife that folded and fit in a soft leather case.
Now — are you sure? he asks, raising an eyebrow,
looking from me to Faith and back. (Did he just wink?)
> *Are you both certain you want to hear*
> *the rest of the story? It does get strange.*

Faith gets her little-girl-big-eyes look.
I stare her down, and she whispers, *Yes.*
Uncle Arthur nods, and then goes on:
> *Peddler Joe didn't sell me that knife. It was not*
> *a gift. I don't think you'd call it a trade,* he says.

I ask, *Well, what was it, then?*
> He answers, *Listen to the rest of the tale.*
> > *Then maybe you'll tell me.*

Uncle Arthur

Thunder rumbling, coming closer.
Lightning flashing in the sky.
Peter, look, Faith whispers, *Uncle Arthur
has a twinkle in his eye.*
Do I, now? Well, we're coming to the tricky part.
Let me try to tell it right.

> *Peddler Joe saw me look at his hand,*
> *curious as Christmas Eve.*
> *"Arthur Armitage," he said, "I'm missing something.*
> *Seem to have lost it around here somewhere*
> *when I traveled this way last year."*
> *He held out his hand. "You see this finger?"*
> > *I said "No,"*
> *and he laughed out loud—that no-finger*
> > *was exactly*
> > *what he was showing me.*

> *Peddler Joe tried to make a deal:*
> *"If you find my finger and give it back,*
> *I'll trade it to you for this pocketknife."*

The one I wanted more
than I'd ever wanted anything
in all my life!

What would you have done? I ask the children.
I'd look for his finger! says Faith right away.
Faith, Peter argues, *seriously?*
It had been a whole year since he lost it!

I have to agree.
Well, yes, I say. *But that's just what I did.*
I went out searching for Peddler Joe's finger.
Up the road and down the other side.
In the hollow tree where the squirrels hid their nuts.
I searched in the basement and up in the attic.
I climbed on a chair to the top pantry shelf,
where my mother kept her secret box.

Peter says, *That's just plain creepy! Why*
would your mother hide some old man's finger?

I can't stop a small chuckle as I go on:
I told no one what I was looking for.

That night I could hardly sleep, thinking
about that knife, determined
to keep on searching — but where?

I got up early and looked some more.
Peddler Joe was leaving that afternoon.
I never stopped thinking. I searched until
the time came when I had to tell him,
          "I'm sorry, Peddler Joe.
                    I can't find your finger."

I pause for a minute.

Faith says, *What?*

          That can't be the end!

Of course it's not.

          And what, I ask, *do you think*
          Peddler Joe did then?

I give them time to think it over.

          How would we know? asks Faith.

          We weren't there, Peter says.

They stare at me until I go on:

          Peddler Joe gave me that knife.

Yes, he did. He put it right here
in the palm of my hand.
Then off he walked down the road
past Lucy's house —
      singing and dancing, she told me later,
           pushing his cart, skipping along,
                  as if he'd just won a million dollars.

It looks like the rain has finally stopped.
The applesauce pot is full to the top.

Lucy's Song

We had no children of our own,
but wherever Arthur sat down,
nieces and nephews and neighbor kids,
and later their children, and cousins and friends,
would gather around to hear him tell
those tales that cast a magic spell.

Peter

I'm heading down the road
on my rattletrap bike,
feet up on the handlebars,
wind through my hair.
When I ride past
Rosie's house,
      she's jumping
      on her trampoline,
      flipping
      in the air.
Bouncing high,
she waves at me
as I come into sight.
I wave back, and—yikes—
my bike tips to the side.
I almost land in a mud puddle,
but luckily not quite.

Faith

Peter got back from his bike ride
about half an hour ago,
and came to sit on the apple-tree bench
with Uncle Arthur and me.
We're quiet together, watching two bluebirds
perched on a low branch.
Now here comes Rosie Timmons, riding her bike
down the road, her red baseball cap
on backwards, black curls poking out. Peter
is trying not to notice, but when her cap
goes flying, he jumps up, runs
to catch it, and gives it back to Rosie.
Her smile is a mile wide
as she hops on her bike. *Thanks!*
she yells, and heads for home.
I wonder if my brother knows
his face is as red as this apple.
I could tease him about it,
but for some reason, I don't.

Uncle Arthur

Peter asks, *Uncle Arthur, what happened*
to the knife you got from Peddler Joe?
I ask if he's still certain he wants to know.
I'm sure, he answers. Faith says she is, too.

        So here I go:
        The night he gave me the pocketknife,
        I took it out of its leather case,
        opened the blade, and tried it out.
        If you look at my old bed upstairs —
        you can still see the nick on the headboard
        where I tested the knife that night.

Faith says, *I've seen that! It's true.*

        And I go on:
        I couldn't sleep. I kept opening
        and closing the knife until,
        to get it out of my sight,
        I slipped it — open — under my pillow.
        And then, at last, I slept.

I look at the two of them, all eyes and ears.
I hold out my hand, and say:

    When I woke up
    the next morning — would you believe it?
    My finger looked
        like it looks today.

Lucy's Song

Oh, the stories I heard him weave—
I never knew quite what to believe.
From the time we were young until we grew old,
I never stopped loving Arthur
    and the stories he told.

Faith

I take Uncle Arthur's hand
     and turn it over.
I study the stump
     of the finger
     where a whole finger should be.
Did you ever see Peddler Joe after that? I ask him.

Uncle Arthur gets a faraway look in his eyes.
Oh, yes, to be sure, I did, he says.
     When Peddler Joe
     came back the next summer,
     what do you think
     was the first thing I saw?

I look at Peter and he looks at me.
You tell us and we'll all know, I say.

Uncle Arthur

Well, I tell Faith and Peter,
I heard the bell on Peddler Joe's cart,
and of course I ran out to meet him.
Like the summer before, he greeted me:
    "Hello, Arthur Armitage."
Yes, he still remembered my name.
        He held out his hand
        and I shook it.

Now, I could hardly believe my eyes,
and you may not believe what I say:
        Peddler Joe
        had four fingers — as well as a thumb —
            on each hand
        that long-ago summer day.

Peter

Uncle Arthur reaches deep down
in his pocket, takes out his silver knife,
and opens its shiny blade.
He picks an apple from the tree,
cuts a slice for Faith, a slice for me,
a slice for himself,
and then another three.

The apple is crisp.
The juice is warm and sweet.
He cuts off one more slice for each of us,
leaving just the core.
> *I'm an old man now,* he says.
> *I don't need this knife anymore.*

I look at the knife. Faith looks at me.
Uncle Arthur looks at the apple tree.
> *Would either of you,* he asks,
> *like to have this knife — to keep?*

Faith

Uncle Arthur's eyes are twinkling
so much it looks like the whole night sky
is shining deep inside him
somewhere we can't quite see.

I watch him chew and swallow
the entire apple core
before I answer:
> *I'll have to think about that a little more.*

Peter

Rosie rides by on her bike again,
her red baseball cap
tilted backwards on her head.

She smiles at me.
          That's right.
          At me.
          This certain way.

I look
from her
to Uncle Arthur.

          I'll take that knife, I stand up and say.

Uncle Arthur

Peter holds the knife in his hands.
Faith looks from him to me and back —
she's taken by surprise. Maybe a little sad.
Ah, yes. There is one more thing I have to add:
>*I've had that knife*
>*for sixty years; it's still as sharp*
>*as the day I first held it. Now*
>*that it's going to be yours, Peter,*
>*here's one more thing you should know:*
>*if you want to keep it shiny and sharp,*
>*you must sleep with it open, under your pillow,*
>*every year — just once a year,*
>*on the night before your birthday.*

His eyes open just a little wider
as he slips the knife back in its case.
And I'm not sure — is that a tiny smile
that flashes across his sister's face?

Faith

Uncle Arthur is leaving tonight.
Peter is carving every piece of wood in sight—
    a bear
    that actually looks like a bear,
    a fish
    that seems to swim through the air.
I climb up high in the apple tree,
and find his initials: *P.C.*
And not far away an *R* and a *T.*

Peter will want to keep that knife
    shiny and sharp
        for the rest of his life.

Uncle Arthur

With seven jars of applesauce
packed in the trunk of my car,
I'm as ready to leave as I'll ever be.
I get in and close the door.

Faith opens the door to give me
one more hug. What can I give
this beautiful girl
that's anywhere near as big
as the gift I gave her brother?

Faith, I say, *I tell you what.*
You keep looking for what really happened,
and next time I come to visit
                 you tell me.

It takes a minute before the stars
light up her eyes.
The start of a story? A little song?
                 And then we'll both know, she says.

Faith

I sit on the bench and watch Uncle Arthur
drive off down the road.
And, as if Aunt Lucy were sitting beside me,
a song starts up in my head:

> *When I was a little child,*
> *no more than two or three,*
> *Aunt Lucy and Uncle Arthur*
> *planted a seed in me.*
>
> *Peter has Uncle Arthur's knife—*
> *he can carve whatever he sees.*
> *I have stories and songs in my life,*
> *like an orchard of apple trees.*

Acknowledgments

Many thanks to family and friends who have helped me write this story. Special thanks to:

— Liz Bicknell, for careful and perceptive editing

— sisters and brothers and parents, for love and memories

— aunts and uncles and nieces and nephews and cousins of several generations

— fellow writers and other friends who have shared the journey

— Amy June Bates, for her delightful illustrations

— Ginger Knowlton, my agent, and everyone at Candlewick who has a hand in turning a story into a book, especially Sarah Ketchersid, Carter Hasegawa, and Allison Hill

— and always, Chad, Lloyd, and Glen.